THE GHOST DOG

...d scientists in stories can ...monsters, can't they? Not ...old boys like Daniel. Well, ...the night of his spooky party, ... and his friends make up ...story about a terrifying dog... ...ry made up to frighten Aaron ..., big-headed Aaron. But to ...horror, what begins as a story ...nto a nightmare. Each night ...st dog – a bloodthirsty, howling ...r – haunts his dreams, and Dan ...s that what he conjured up ...his imagination has somehow ...e... real!

THE
GHOST DOG

Pete Johnson

Illustrated by Peter Dennis

First published in 1996 by
Corgi Yearling Books
This Large Print edition published by
BBC Audiobooks Ltd
by arrangement with Corgi Yearling
Books, a division of the Random House
Group Ltd
2005

ISBN 1 4056 6028 7

British Library Cataloguing in Publication Data available

Johnson, Pete, 1956-
  The ghost dog.—Large print ed.
  1. Children's stories 2. Large type books
  I. Title
  823. 9'14[J]

ISBN 1-4056-6028-7

Printed and bound in Great Britain by
Antony Rowe Ltd., Chippenham, Wiltshire

The Ghost Dog is dedicated to
Jan, Linda, Robin and Harry;
Rose, Jack and Freddie Jewitt;
Jo and Laura May;
Alex and Grant Harnett

With grateful thanks.

CHAPTER ONE

The first time I only saw its face.

Out of the darkness it came floating towards me.

It had evil red eyes.

Blood poured out of its mouth.

It was the ugliest, most horrible thing I had ever seen.

And I'd brought it to life.

I'd thought it was only mad scientists in stories who could create monsters. Not ten-year-old boys like me: Daniel Grant.

Don't ask me how I did it. I'm still not sure. I certainly never meant it to

1

appear at my spooky party.

* * *

It was Laura's idea to have a party for Halloween.

She first mentioned it after school when we were taking Rocky for a walk. Rocky is my pet rat.

At first I'd wanted a dog but my mum wouldn't let me. So then I went to the pet shop and saw this albino rat in a cage. And he looked at me so imploringly I knew he wanted me to buy him. So I did. Now I reckon he's the best pet you can have.

Every day after school he snuggles down my shirt while Laura and I take him to the common. There we let him run around. He loves that but he never tries to get away. In fact, he can be a bit of a pain because he wants to be stroked all the time.

Rocky was licking orange off our fingers when I started yawning again.

'You've been yawning all day,' said Laura.

'I know,' I said. 'It's because . . .' I

hesitated. I didn't want to tell anyone and yet I did. Perhaps I would just tell Laura.

By the way, people are always calling Laura my girlfriend and I know they say it as a kind of joke but it really annoys me.

Laura and I often go fishing as well as kick-boxing every Wednesday. She's an excellent goal-keeper and never seems to mind being the only girl when we play football. In fact, I think she likes it. She's quite small with dark brown hair and a quiet whispery voice, although she can shout when she wants to. She's my best mate and she has been ever since we met at infant school.

So then I told her. 'You know on the news they said about that man who'd escaped from prison?'

'The one with the really mean face,' began Laura.

'That's him,' I said. 'Well, I didn't get much sleep last night because I kept hearing these noises and I was sure he was hiding in my attic.'

Laura's eyes grew bigger. 'And what was it?'

'Rocky jumping up and down in his cage,' I replied. 'At least I think that's what it was.' We both laughed nervously, then I started stroking Rocky. 'When I was younger, a lot younger,' I went on, 'I used to arrange my toy soldiers so that all their guns were pointing at the door. Then some nights I'd put my tanks out too . . . I still like to have something by my bed even if it's only a tennis racket, just in case.' I paused.

There was silence for a moment before Laura said, quietly, 'What I hate is when that man at the end of *Crimewatch* says, "Sleep well tonight and don't have any bad dreams, will

4

you?" And I think, it's all right for you in your nice, comfy studio with about two hundred people around you, but I'm on my own upstairs . . . some nights I'll be thinking about what he's said so much, that I have to go and switch my light on and stand in the light for a little while.' She shivered and smiled. 'It's Halloween next week.'

'I know.'

'We must do something,' she said. 'And not trick or treat. Last year everyone was doing that. No, we ought to have a proper party where we can play *Murder in the Dark*.'

'I love *Murder in the Dark*,' I cried.

'And afterwards we could all sit round and tell really gory stories,' she said. We looked at each other excitedly. Then Laura sighed. 'Only my dad would never let me have a party like that.'

I silently agreed. Laura's dad's all right but he gets stressed very easily. Like yesterday, he made Laura go up to her room just because he found her shoes down by the sofa.

'There's always my house,' I said.

'Do you think your mum would let you?' asked Laura.

'It depends what sort of mood she's in, but I think I can talk her round, especially if I get Roy on my side.' Roy

is my mum's boyfriend.

But in the end I didn't need Roy's support. To my total surprise Mum said 'Yes', rightaway.

'How many friends can I invite?' I asked.

'About six,' suggested Mum.

'Not counting Laura.'

Mum smiled. 'Not counting Laura . . . and we'll have to keep an eye on Carrie. We don't want her getting scared.'

Carrie is my seven-year-old sister. 'Nothing scares her,' I said.

Next day Laura and I worked out who we were going to invite. Top of both our lists was Harry, because he's mad. He really is. I mean, I've never seen anyone laugh like Harry. He's got this really loud laugh and when he starts he just can't stop: tears fall down his face and he always leans too far back on his chair and falls over. Then, because he's laughing so much he can't get up again, which winds teachers up something rotten. It's brilliant to see.

Next to Laura, Harry is probably my best mate. He got really excited about the Halloween party. So did everyone else we invited. Then, two days before Halloween, came shock news.

'I know you're going to be disappointed,' said Mum, 'but I'm afraid we're going to have to cancel the Halloween party.'

I looked up sharply. 'Why?'

Mum became embarrassed. 'Well, Roy's been offered this job which means he'll be away on business a lot in America over the next few months, so he's asked if Aaron could stay here with us and make a fresh start.'

Aaron is Roy's son. I'd only seen him about twice but that was enough. He

just loves himself; a total bighead. Mum went rattling on. 'So Aaron will be moving in on Friday night. I know that's when we'd planned your party but I can't manage a party on that night as well. Don't worry, though, I will make it up to you.'

'Don't bother,' I muttered.

'Oh come on, Dan, we'll do something special soon, I promise,' said Mum. 'Got any ideas?'

'Yeah, a Halloween party,' I said. 'That's all I want.'

I was so angry about my party being cancelled it was only later I realized what else it meant: my home was going to be invaded. By Aaron.

Ever since my dad walked out, it had just been my mum, Carrie and me and I'd got to like that. I certainly didn't want it changed now.

'Why has Aaron got to come here?' I demanded. 'Why can't he go to his nan's or . . . ?'

'Because I want to do this for Roy,' interrupted Mum. 'It's a decision I've made and that's that.' She had a real 'Don't argue with me' look on her face.

Then she added, a bit more gently, 'It is the right thing to do. Later you'll see that.'

She was smiling at me now. I turned away. Then I thought of something. 'And where's he going to sleep?'

'I can't see him sharing with Carrie, can you?' replied Mum, trying to make a little joke of it all. 'And you have got the biggest bedroom.'

But as I said to Laura later, that doesn't mean Mum can just move someone into my room without even asking me. How would she like it if I told her I was bunging another woman into her bedroom.

'She wouldn't like it at all,' agreed Laura. 'And I'd really hate to share my room with a stranger,' she added.

'This Aaron's ruined everything,' I said, 'including our Halloween party.'

*   *   *

It was about half-past-seven on Halloween night when Roy and Aaron arrived in this big van. The first thing Aaron unpacked was this new

10

mountain bike, which his dad had just bought for him. I think I'm lucky if my dad sends me a five-pound gift token at Christmas.

Then Mum said to me, 'Show your guest where he's staying.'

I wanted to say, 'He's not my guest,' but I didn't, as earlier Mum had given me this pep talk. 'Now, you must make Aaron feel welcome: remember, his mum's passed away and it can't be easy for him, new home, new school . . .' So I did try and twist my face into a smile as I went up the stairs with him. But watching him pile his suitcases into my room gave me this really tight pain in my stomach.

Aaron prowled around my room and didn't look at all impressed. He

pointed at Rocky in his cage. 'You've got a pet rat.' He sounded mocking.

'He's called Rocky—and he lives here,' I added, in case Aaron was going to say he couldn't share a room with a pet rat.

But instead, Aaron picked up the scarf I'd put on top of the bunk bed—just so he'd know that was my place. 'So you're a Spurs supporter,' he said.

'Yeah, what about you?'

'Arsenal is the only team worth supporting.' He turned around and glared at me. He'd had his hair shaved really short round the sides; I think he was trying to look hard. But he was actually very skinny and quite small, half a head smaller than me, even though he was a year older.

Then Mum, Roy and Carrie all tumbled into my room.

'Getting settled in all right, Aaron?' asked my mum. 'Daniel's made space for you, so there should be plenty of room.'

'Oh yes, plenty of room,' said Roy, rubbing his hands together. Then he laughed loudly, showing all his white pointy teeth. He had his arm all round Mum's shoulder. I hate it when seriously old people do things like that.

At first Carrie was skipping around him excitedly. But later, when we were all sitting downstairs having sandwiches, she just sat on Mum's lap, not talking to anyone. Aaron and I didn't say much either.

It was just Mum and Roy who were babbling away. Roy was wearing his usual leather jacket and jeans. He rides a Harley Davidson motorbike and has taken me out on it a few times. I guess he's pretty good to me, although he's never bought me a mountain bike. He said to me, 'I'm sorry you had to postpone your Halloween party.'

'It doesn't matter,' I said, quietly.

'Yes, it does,' said Roy, firmly. 'We're still going to have it, you know.'

'A Halloween party has to be on Halloween,' I muttered.

'OK, well, we'll just call it something else, like . . .'

I looked up. 'A spooky party.'

'Brilliant,' he said. 'And we'll make this party even scarier than Halloween.

We can get some plastic skeletons from the joke shop and some masks and . . .'

'When?' I interrupted.

Roy turned to Mum. 'I'm back from the States two weeks tonight, so how about holding it then?'

She nodded, smiling. 'Why not?' She turned to Aaron. 'Do you like spooky parties?'

Aaron just shrugged and looked bored.

'Of course he does,' said his dad, heartily. 'Make out some proper invitations, Daniel,' he went on: 'After

14

all, everyone has Halloween parties but spooky parties are much more special.'

'We'll do the invitations tomorrow,' I said. 'Me and Laura,' I added, just in case anyone thought I'd meant me and Aaron.

Next morning I woke up very early. And straightaway I heard it, the noise which had been waking me up all night: Aaron breathing really noisily and deeply through his mouth. It was as if he were trying to suck up all the air in my bedroom, leaving none for me.

I crept down the ladder from my bed. At least I still had the top bunk. Then I went over to Rocky's cage. At once he was pressing his nose through the cage, eager to say 'Hello'. I let him lick my fingers while whispering to him. Then I turned around and saw I was being watched. Aaron was sitting up in bed, staring at me without saying anything.

'All right?' I muttered.

'All right,' he muttered back. And that was all we said until I fled to the bathroom.

Mum thought Aaron and I were

INVITATION
BE THERE OR BEWARE

IT'S SPOOKY PARTY NIGHT

ENJOY THE FRIGHT

AT: DANIEL'S CRYPT
ALSO KNOWN AS
22 WOODSIDE ROAD

ON:
FRIDAY 14TH NOVEMBER

TIME: 7 O'CLOCK

WARNING:
NOT FOR THE FAINT-HEARTED.

going to walk to school together. But as soon as we got out of the front door we set off on opposite sides of the road. Luckily he wasn't in the same class as me. At lunchtime I saw him on the back field with some guys from his class, but he totally ignored me.

At home we pretty much ignored each other too. Mum remarked about how quiet he was. 'You'd hardly know he was here,' she said. Yet, he was here: watching television and continually flicking the channels to teletext; leaving his clothes and his shoes and hair gel all over my room; cluttering up the house with his mountain bike; and, worst of all, he had a way of looking at me which I came to hate: somehow he could put me down without saying a word.

Then, the day before my spooky party, Aaron did something which really infuriated me. I'd had to leave school early to go to the dentist. So it was after five o'clock when I finally called round at Laura's. To my surprise Harry was there too, and for once he wasn't smiling. Both he and Laura

17

looked very serious.

'What's the matter with you two?'
I asked.

'Nothing, only . . .' began Harry.
Then he looked at Laura. 'Come on,
we've got to tell him.'

'Tell me what?' I cried.

'After school today,' started Laura,
'we went to McDonald's and Aaron
was there with some boys from his
class . . .'

'He was showing off so much I
wanted to punch him,' interrupted
Harry.

'What was he saying?' I asked.

'Oh, just going on and on about all

the things he'd done. I didn't really listen,' said Harry, dismissively. 'But then he came over to Laura and me and said he'd buy us both Big Macs if we liked.'

I stared at him disbelievingly. 'He did what?'

'And he was all smiles,' said Laura. 'Kept going on about how he had the money so it was no trouble.'

I clenched my hands into fists. At once I knew what Aaron's game was: he was trying to steal my friends away from me. 'So what did you do?' I asked, my voice starting to shake.

'We said no, of course,' said Harry. 'We didn't want anything from him. He's just a show-off.'

'You can't buy friends,' added Laura, softly.

I shot her a grateful look, but then I started thinking about Aaron again. 'I really hate people like him,' I whispered, fiercely, 'who are just so full of themselves, they try and take over everything.'

'He deserves a lesson,' said Harry.

I looked at Laura and Harry, then

said, slowly, 'At the spooky party tomorrow, we've got to scare him . . .'

'Yeah,' cried Harry at once.

'And we won't just scare him a bit,' I continued. 'Let's give him the biggest shock of his life.'

CHAPTER TWO

It was at seven o'clock I turned into a zombie: a zombie who has just been woken from the dead and isn't too happy about it.

Mum put fake blood all over my face and we found some really old raggy clothes. Then I sprayed this cobweb stuff over me. I thought I looked pretty good, actually.

Then Laura and Harry turned up. Harry was a werewolf: he had a brilliant mask with hair all coming off it and on his left hand he was wearing this furry glove which looked just like a claw. While Laura had come as a hunchback: she'd made her face very pale, put dust over some old clothes and, of course, she had a cushion up her back.

'You three do look a state,' said Mum. We took this as a huge compliment.

'What do you think of Laura, then?' I asked Harry.

'A big improvement,' he said. 'Actually, I really wanted to come as a poltergeist.'

'But how would you have done that?' asked Laura.

'Don't know,' said Harry. 'That's why I didn't come as one.' He began to laugh.

'You're mad,' said Laura.

'That's true,' he agreed.

Then the front door opened and Aaron shot up the stairs, carrying a large package.

'What's he got in there?' asked Harry.

I shrugged my shoulders.

'Go and have a look; after all, he's in your room,' said Harry.

'No, I don't want to make him feel too important,' I replied.

A couple of minutes later we all saw what was in the parcel: Aaron sauntered back down the stairs in this brand new Spiderman costume. He started strutting over to us.

'That must have cost a bomb,' exclaimed Harry.

And Mum said to Roy, 'I thought the children were making their own costumes for this party.'

'Oh, I'd promised Aaron a Spiderman costume ages ago,' replied Roy. 'It's just, tonight, I finally got round to buying it. Doesn't he look great?'

Mum didn't answer, instead, she charged back into the kitchen. Roy rushed after her, while Aaron just stood there as if frozen to the spot.

'Look at him,' I muttered. 'He thinks he's so great.'

'It's much better to make your own costume,' said Laura.

'Of course it is,' I said. Yet I couldn't help thinking how shabby and cheap my costume looked against Aaron's. His was a deluxe costume; mine looked as if it was out of the bargain basement.

'It's a cheat buying a costume,' I

cried, loud enough for Aaron to hear. 'He shouldn't be allowed into my party like that.'

Aaron took a couple of steps towards me. 'I see you've come as yourself,' he hissed. 'An idiot.'

'Ignore him,' whispered Laura.

But I was already squaring up to him. 'What about you,' I taunted. 'Daddy's little pet.'

Now we were facing each other just as if we were about to have a fight. I really think there would have been a fight if Roy hadn't burst in, yelling, 'Come on everyone, let's get busy. We haven't long to make this house scary, you know.'

So we charged about putting black sheeting over the porch, hanging up a skeleton just inside the doorway and changing the light in the hallway to orange, as that was spookier. Then Mum, who had taken Carrie off to stay with a friend, returned and Roy kept smiling at her and asking her what she thought of everything.

Soon the guests started arriving, shouting and giggling excitedly in their masks. Then Roy organized some games like apple bobbing and eating a doughnut off a piece of string, and the treasure hunt.

For the treasure hunt we had to go out into the garden and find these bags of gold coins which Mum and Roy had hooked on to the bushes and trees. 'Remember the pond is out of bounds,' Mum called after us. Last time we'd played this game, someone had fallen in the pond. It was so funny.

We tore around the garden in twos and threes. Only Aaron was on his own. Everyone was whispering about him though, and what a 'big show-off' he was, wearing that Spiderman costume tonight.

'So when are we going to scare Aaron?' asked Harry.

'After tea, when we play *Murder in the Dark*, and there are no grown-ups around,' I said. 'We'll do something, then, for sure.'

But I still wasn't certain what, exactly. We trooped back inside for tea. There were burgers with lots of ketchup on, which I called 'Blood

Burgers', spider cakes which had icing in the shape of a spider's web on top, jellies with plastic spiders in them . . . there was just so much food. The only trouble was it took such a long time to eat, that by the time we'd finished it was almost the end of the party.

'I don't think we've got enough time to play *Murder in the Dark*,' said Mum.

But I was determined. 'We've got to play *Murder in the Dark*, haven't we?' I cried. I looked at Harry and Laura, who immediately backed me up. And soon the whole party was chanting: 'We want *Murder in the Dark*. We want *Murder in the Dark*.'

'All right,' said Mum, finally. 'Everyone into the lounge.'

We huddled around Mum and Roy. Mum took out this pack of cards. 'Now, I'm going to pass the cards around. Don't, whatever you do, turn your card over yet.' There was a tense silence as Mum handed around the cards. 'Now you may turn your card over,' she said. 'Remember, whoever gets the Ace of Spades is the murderer.'

I gazed at my card with a mixture of astonishment and excitement.

For the first time ever, I had the Ace of Spades.

'Who has got the Ace of Spades?' asked my mum.

'I have,' I cried, holding the card right up in the air.

'Then tonight you are the murderer,' said Mum, handing me the rubber dagger. I grinned around while my heart was thumping wildly. I saw Laura and Harry looking eagerly at me. And I knew what they were thinking: get Aaron.

No-one ever wants to be the first person caught: it's like saying, 'I'm a geek.' So I was determined to catch Aaron first tonight.

'Now you've all got just five minutes to hide from our murderer.'

I gave an evil laugh while twisting the dagger around in my hand. 'You've all got five minutes to live.'

'Just one last thing,' said Mum. 'The hall light has to be left on at all times, all right?' Everyone nodded solemnly. 'Right, then, off you go,' she cried. And at once everyone rushed off, Harry and Laura giving me another look as they left.

'Just listen to them,' grinned Roy. And it did sound as if there was a herd of mad rhinos charging about upstairs —only rhinos who kept laughing and yelling hysterically.

Mum looked at her stop-watch. 'Two minutes left,' she called. The sounds upstairs were quieter and more muffled now.

'Hey, why don't we join in this?' cried Roy suddenly.

'Well, we've only fifty-four seconds left,' said Mum.

'That's plenty of time,' grinned Roy and with that he grabbed Mum's hand and they rushed away, Mum handing me the stop-watch as she left.

I watched Mum and Roy race up the stairs. Then, by a piece of good fortune, I glimpsed someone else run downstairs. Aaron.

But I played fair. I turned my back and counted off the last seconds on the stop-watch.

So Aaron was hiding downstairs. I wondered where he'd go. And then I was certain I knew: he'd hide in the laundry basket under the stairs.

For that's where I used to hide. It was a bit smelly in that laundry basket, especially if any of my old socks were in there. But it was a superb hiding place, and no-one ever looked there. No

30

doubt Aaron thought he was really clever thinking of it. Well, I'd soon wipe the smug smile off his face.

Time was up. My first idea was just to charge over to the laundry basket. But then I decided, to add atmosphere, I'd switch the hall light off first. I know Mum had said to keep the light on, but I wanted to really scare Aaron.

So I switched off the orange light, then stared around me, letting my eyes get used to the darkness. It suddenly seemed to get colder. I shivered. And then I saw it creeping towards me. It looked like a large dog or something. It must be someone on their hands and knees.

Aaron.

He's realized I'm on to his hiding place and is trying to sneak past me.

All at once I charged forward with my rubber dagger . . . and then let out the most terrible cry of pain you've ever heard. For I'd tripped over something and fallen splat on to my face. As I tried to get up this terrible pain shot up from my ankle. As I wobbled to my feet the pain became sharper. I let out another cry. I couldn't help it. Then I heard a door burst open and Roy calling down the stairs: 'What's going on down there?' At that same moment the doorbell rang.

Footsteps raced downstairs and I heard my mum's voice exclaiming: 'Who switched the light out? I know the switch is around here somewhere,' while the doorbell rang again, twice this time.

Then all at once the hall was full of orange light again and Mum, Roy, and two very worried-looking parents were all staring at me.

32

'I fell over,' I gasped, looking downwards at the box in which we'd put all the rubbish from the party. 'I fell over a box,' I added helpfully.

'I told you to leave that hall light on,' cried Mum. I had a feeling this wouldn't be the last time I'd hear her say that tonight.

Now everyone was jostling downstairs to see what was happening: and what was happening was me feeling more than a bit stupid.

Just before I hobbled away to the kitchen with Mum I watched 'Spiderman' slowly clamber out of the laundry basket.

I gaped at him incredulously. It can't have been Aaron I'd spotted in the darkness.

So who or what was it?

I shivered again.

CHAPTER THREE

'I told you not to switch the hall light off . . . but as usual, you have to go your own way. Well, what happened serves you right.'

'Number four,' I murmured to myself. There was no point in arguing with Mum; that only got her even madder. And besides, she was right; it was my own fault. So all I could do was keep score of the number of times Mum nagged me while she strapped up my ankle.

Would she top her all-time record of seven 'nags' in one hour? Not tonight.

In fact, when she saw me limping around the kitchen she threw away the record and said, 'You're not a bad boy really, just a bit headstrong. It's a shame your party had to end like that.' Then to cheer me up she said I could go out to the hut in the garden with Laura and Harry (they were sleeping over; all my other guests had gone home long ago) and tell scary stories.

I popped upstairs to get Rocky. Aaron was there, lying on the bottom bunk in his Spiderman outfit. I just wanted to go over to him and punch him in the face. I had a feeling he wanted to do the same to me. But instead, we totally ignored each other. Then I ran downstairs and went out to the hut at the bottom of the garden where Laura and Harry were already waiting for me. It was pitch dark in there except for the light from the torch which Mum had given Harry. Rocky jumped on to Laura's shoulder and started cleaning himself.

It was quite a small hut which reeked of mustiness and stale grass from the lawn-mower in the corner. There was just one tiny window patterned with cobwebs. I squashed down between Laura—who was now sitting on her hump—and Harry. Then, before anyone else could say it, I declared, 'I made a right fool of myself tonight.'

'That's true,' said Harry, grinning at me.

'And we certainly scared Aaron, didn't we?' sighed Laura.

'All right, all right,' I muttered. 'I really thought he was . . . it was so weird.'

'What was?' asked Laura.

'When I switched the hall light off, I

saw this shape moving towards me. At first I thought it was Aaron on his hands and knees, and then . . . well it could have been a dog: a massive dog.'

'Like that Irish wolfhound we used to see,' said Harry. 'Remember it?'

'Oh yes,' cried Laura. 'It used to terrify me it was so big. It would suddenly tear out of those flats by the school.'

'And its owner was this really little guy,' said Harry. 'We used to say that dog was his bodyguard.'

'Too right,' I said. 'No-one would mess with that dog, yank your leg off as soon as look at you, that one. No wonder it always looked so superior.'

'And sometimes we'd hear it behind us,' murmured Laura, 'because it used to breathe really heavily . . . Oh, I was so glad when that man and his dog moved away.'

'Only tonight, it came back,' said Harry, 'as the ghost dog.' He shone the torch right into my face. 'Of course, you could be making this all up.'

'No, I'm not. I swear on your life.'

'On my life,' exclaimed Harry.

'Joke. No, I swear on my life I did see something.'

'We'll believe you,' said Harry. 'Millions wouldn't.' He swung the torch away from me and around the hut. As it alighted on to the door, the handle began to move. I could sense Laura and Harry tensing beside me. Harry kept the torch on the door handle, as it turned again.

'I don't like this,' whispered Laura.

'Maybe it's your ghost dog,' muttered Harry, 'wanting to be taken for a walk.' We laughed nervously.

Suddenly the door sprang open and Roy and Aaron were staring in at us. Roy gave one of his hearty laughs. 'Did we scare you then?'

'No, not at all,' said Harry and me.

'Just a bit,' whispered Laura.

'All right if we join you?' asked Roy. I groaned inwardly. But Roy was already squeezing in beside me. As always, he smelt of too much soap.

'Come on, Aaron, room for one more,' called Roy. His tone was light-hearted but it was an order just the same.

Aaron squashed down beside his dad. He looked awkward and angry. He'd changed out of his Spiderman costume and was just wearing his usual T-shirt and jeans now.

'So what are we doing, all telling chilling stories?' Roy winked at us. I liked Roy, he could be a good bloke. But I did think at times he tried too hard to be one of the gang. He didn't seem to realize there were certain events at which adults weren't

welcome. And ghost-telling events was one of them. How could you tell really bloodthirsty, gory tales with a grown-up there?

'Aaron knows some good ghost stories,' began Roy.

'No, I don't,' interrupted Aaron rudely.

'Yes, you do, Aaron. Come on, share them with your friends.'

Aaron glared at his dad. 'Just leave it, all right,' he whispered.

Roy stirred angrily and there was an awkward silence until Harry declared, 'Well, I know a spooky story, want to hear it?' Laura, Roy and I nodded eagerly.

'It all began one dark and gloomy night,' said Harry, 'when this woman, who's in the house all on her own, gets a phone call. This really husky voice says to her: "Hello, I am Blood Fingers and I'm coming to get you." The woman put the phone down, shaking. Then a minute later the phone rings again and she hears that horrible, husky voice say, "I am Blood Fingers and I am at your gate." The phone keeps ringing and each time he is getting closer. "I am Blood Fingers and I am in your garden. I am Blood

40

Fingers and I am at your door" and then . . . "I am Blood Fingers and I am in your house and I know where you are. I can see you. I am standing right next to you." The woman turns round and there is this huge guy with blood all over his hands. "Hello," he goes, "I'm Blood Fingers. You haven't got any plasters, have you?"'

At once, Harry burst into peals of laughter. And it was hard not to join in. Even Aaron laughed faintly.

'You really had me going there,' Roy said to Harry. He grinned broadly.

'Laura's turn now,' joked Harry.

'Oh, I can't think,' began Laura, 'my mind's gone blank. They do say, if at midnight on Halloween night you comb your hair a hundred times, then stare hard into the mirror, you'll see the face of the person you're going to marry.'

'That's not scary,' I said.

'Depends who you see,' said Harry.

'There's a story,' went on Laura, 'that a man did this and then he saw a vampire in his mirror which ripped his face open.'

'Nice,' murmured Harry.

Roy got up. 'I expect I'll be told off if I don't give a hand with the drying-up. So I'll leave you to it. I enjoyed your story, Harry.' Then, in a piercing whisper to Aaron, 'And don't be afraid to join in.'

Even I couldn't help feeling a bit embarrassed for Aaron at that moment. There's nothing worse than a parent who tries to push you into things.

I think Laura felt a bit sorry for Aaron, too, because she said, quite gently to him, 'Would you like to have a go at telling a ghost story now?'

Aaron didn't answer for a moment. Then he said in this really sneery voice,

'I stopped telling ghost stories years ago. They never scared me anyway . . .'

I was so angry I couldn't speak at first. Why did Aaron always have to act as if he was way above us? He ruined everything. Then Harry looked across at me. 'There's one ghost story which scares everyone, isn't there, Dan . . . a true one, too?'

I hadn't a clue what Harry was talking about, but I went along with him. 'Yeah, that's a terrible story, but we'd better not tell Aaron that one; it would only give him nightmares.'

Aaron gave a mocking laugh.

'Will you tell Aaron the story or shall I?' asked Harry.

'I will,' I said. 'This is the true story of . . . of the ghost dog.' And as I said those words, my heart began to beat excitedly. I switched off the torch so the whole place was in darkness.

A picture was forming at the back of my head. And as it became clearer I felt this strange power building up inside me. 'This is an old, local legend,' I began, my voice shaking slightly with excitement. 'There was this boy who lived with his parents and they were quite poor. One night the boy goes downstairs to get some biscuits when he finds a dead dog in his basement.'

'Aaah, that's sad,' murmured Laura.

'But suddenly the dog springs to life, and it's the biggest dog the boy has ever seen: an Irish wolfhound. But he tells the boy not to be afraid, and says: "If you do me a favour I'll do you one. Will you make me a grave where I can rest. If you do that I'll give you a hundred pounds."

'The boy's eyes open wide when he hears about the hundred pounds and he asks for the money rightaway. "All right, I'll trust you," says the dog and he gets the boy to follow him. They walk into the deepest part of the old churchyard and then the dog asks the boy to lift a large stone up. The boy does so and underneath the stone are ten ten-pound notes. The boy stares at the money in amazement. He's never had so much money in his life before.

' "Now I can go to the fair," he cries.

' "Don't forget your part of the bargain," the dog calls after him.

' "No, I'll be back tonight to make your grave, I promise," cries the boy.

' "I'll be here," says the dog and with a little sigh he sits down and waits . . . and waits. But the boy has such a good time at the fair with his mates, that he forgets all about the dog.

'But later that night the boy hears strange scratching noises in his bedroom. And then he sees a pair of red eyes staring at him. It is the dog. "You broke your promise to me," he says. "Now I shall make sure you never forget me. I am going to haunt your

45

dreams for the rest of your life."

'And that is what the dog did. Every night when the boy closed his eyes the dog was waiting for him; and each night the dog became more monstrous and terrifying. Until, one morning, his parents found the boy dead in his bed. And on his face was a look of such terror . . . he had been literally frightened to death by the ghost dog.'

I paused. That story had seemed so real to me I'd lost myself in it, even shuddering at the end. But had it scared Aaron? All at once, there was loud, mocking laughter.

'What a load of old rubbish,' said Aaron.

'It's not rubbish,' I replied fiercely. 'It's real.'

Then Harry said, 'Come on Danny, you haven't told Aaron the end of the story, have you?'

'You tell him the rest, then,' I replied, wondering what Harry was up to.

'Well,' said Harry. 'The end of the story is this: the dog has to go off and make its own grave. It digs a hole, then it carries some stones to cover up the grave. And even though the stones make the dog's mouth bleed, it goes on getting the stones. And finally, the dog finished making his grave, its mouth full of blood. And the dog said that if anyone took so much as one stone away from his grave he would haunt them for ever.'

'And do you know where he is buried?' said Laura, picking up the story now. 'Just up the road by the old church. Of course, I'd be too scared to even move a stone, let alone take one away. That place really gives me the creeps. But . . . you wouldn't be scared, would you, Aaron?' Then she added, slyly, 'So why don't you take a stone away?'

'What, now?' whispered Aaron. Suddenly, his voice seemed to have shrunk.

'Yes, why not now?' I said. 'You don't believe in any of it, do you?'

'Go on, I dare you,' said Laura.

'So do I,' joined in Harry.

All three of us stared at him expectantly. We had him cornered. He sat very still as if he were playing statues.

'But we'd never be allowed to go out now,' he said, at last. He was trying to sound tough again, but his voice was shaking all over the place.

'You leave that to me,' I said. 'Now, will you go through with it or do you want to chicken out?'

'I never chicken out of anything,' he whispered.

'Right, well I'll just go and get us permission.' I sprang to my feet, forgetting all about my twisted ankle. The pain made me wince for a moment. Then I limped into the kitchen. Roy was putting some glasses

away in the cupboard. He turned and smiled at me.

'How's it all going?' he asked.

'Well, we've been telling Aaron the ghost story about the old church down the road and now he's really keen to see it.'

'What, now?' exclaimed Roy. 'Bit late, isn't it?'

'It's just Aaron's so keen.' And from my tone of voice you'd have thought Aaron and I had become very chummy.

Roy considered for a moment. 'Well, it's good Aaron is joining in at last. I suppose a quick look would be all right. I'll have to come with you, of course, but I'll try not to cramp your style.'

I rushed back to tell the others. Laura and Harry looked really excited; Aaron kept his face blank. But I knew he was getting scared and that made me very happy.

Then Mum appeared. 'I don't think you should go walking on that ankle,' she said.

'It's fine now,' I lied. 'And Roy said we could,' I added. Mum gave Roy one of her looks and muttered about this being a daft time to go out, but she didn't stop us.

The streets were all lit up with pale orange lights, but most of the houses we passed were in darkness. And there

was this eerie silence which made my skin tingle.

The path leading to the old church was so narrow we had to walk in single file. At the end of the path was an old gate. It opened with a creaky sigh, and above it was a message. We all peered intently at it thinking it might be something bloodcurdling, like: THIS CHURCHYARD IS HAUNTED. GO ON IF YOU DARE. But it just said: PLEASE CONTROL YOUR DOGS.

'Doesn't say anything about controlling your rats though, does it?' I said. I stole a glance at Rocky who had snuggled down my arm. 'So Rocky, you can go wild tonight if you like.'

Roy shone his torch ahead of him. 'See, there's the church,' he said. And nestling behind all the trees was a grey stone church.

'But this church is positively ancient,' cried Roy, excitedly. 'I don't think I've ever seen such an old church.' He sprang forward with his torch, then turned back when he saw we weren't following him.

'All right if we go off and explore?'

I asked.

'Just for a few minutes then,' he said doubtfully, 'but stay in sight.' Then he added, 'This church is a real piece of history, you know.' We nodded politely but didn't follow him.

Laura whispered to me, 'What if there aren't any old stones here?'

'There must be some,' I replied, confidently.

We walked up the gravelly path. 'We should have brought another torch,' I muttered. 'It's really hard to see much.' The trees were swaying majestically above us, and I could hear the long grass stirring in the wind.

Suddenly, Harry called, 'Look at this!' He was pointing at a tree, whose trunk was bent right over. It was really weird. Even Aaron couldn't help staring at it.

'Wind must have caught it,' said Harry.

'It looks as if it's been shot,' said Laura. 'There's something very sad about this tree.' Two lorries rumbled noisily past and for a moment lit up that mysterious tree. That's when we saw what was lying around the tree: hundreds of stones.

'That's the spot,' cried Harry, at once.

'Yeah, that's it all right,' I replied. I couldn't have been more excited if we'd discovered gold. I looked at Aaron. 'This is the spot where the dog made his grave and he said if anyone took so much as a stone away he would haunt them for ever. That's why there are so many stones here. No-one has dared remove one until . . . until . . .' Something was behind me.

A huge shadow.

The shadow spoke. 'Good evening.' I whirled around to see this elderly man out with his dog, a little white terrier.

'Good evening,' I whispered.

I think his sudden appearance had given us all a start. We watched him totter away. Then Harry said, briskly, 'Now Aaron, we dare you to take away one of these stones.'

A passing car lit up Aaron's face for a second. He looked pretty sick, actually. But he just said, 'All right, if this is what you want me to do, if it means so much to you.' And there was no hiding the bitterness in his voice. For a moment I felt ashamed, as if we had no business forcing Aaron to do this. But the feeling quickly disappeared.

Aaron bent down, hesitated, then picked up this stone: one of the oddest-looking stones there, shaped like a bone.

Aaron stood staring down at the stone in his hand, as if he didn't know what it was. Then, from faraway came the sound of a dog howling: high and mournful. At once, Aaron's hand started to shake violently, as if the stone was burning him. He let the stone fall out of his hand and on to

the ground. But even after he'd let the stone drop, Aaron's hand was still shaking.

'I'm not messing about with this,' he cried. He sounded dead scared. Then he ran away from us and over towards his dad.

For a moment, we were too stunned to speak. Finally, Laura cried, 'We've done it.'

'It's just amazing,' said Harry, his face one big grin. 'He was so big-headed in the hut, saying all ghost stories were a load of rubbish . . . and then he comes out here and just flips.'

We all smiled at each other triumphantly.

'Did you see the way his hand was shaking when he picked up that stone?' exclaimed Laura.

'And he reckoned he was such a hard man,' I said. 'We've blown his cover all right, haven't we?'

'He's nothing really, is he?' said Harry. All three of us were laughing excitedly now.

'Hurry up you three,' cried Roy suddenly. He didn't sound any too happy. I wondered if he had guessed what we'd been up to.

'I think we should take a stone away,' said Laura.

'Good idea,' I replied. 'It'll be something to show our friend Aaron, won't it?'

Then we all hesitated: 'So who's going to pick the stone up then?' I asked.

Laura suddenly bent down and picked up the same stone Aaron had held a few minutes ago. 'There,' she gasped, 'I've done it.'

As she spoke, that dog howled again, louder and more mournfully than before. She laughed a little breathlessly. 'Come on, let's have some fun with this stone.'

CHAPTER FOUR

It was Laura's idea.

She would take the stone with her into Carrie's bedroom. Then, half an hour later, she would run on to the landing claiming she'd just seen the ghost dog. Harry and I would make a big fuss and see if we could get Aaron scared again.

With anyone else we would have stopped by now. But having discovered Aaron's weakness it was too exhilarating not to go on.

Harry was on a camp bed in my room, and kept whispering about

57

tonight's events. Every so often Harry would do an impression of a chicken and we'd both start giggling. Aaron ignored all our antics. He pretended he was asleep. But I knew he wasn't. I looked at my watch; any second now Laura would run out of her bedroom.

Just then I heard a bedroom door open and footsteps walking across the landing. I lay waiting for Laura to start crying out about the terrible ghost dog she'd seen. But nothing happened. I sat up in bed. 'Harry,' I whispered.

There was no answer. 'Harry, you're not asleep, are you?'

'No, I'm not asleep,' muttered Harry.

But he was speaking really slowly; he sounded as if he were talking at the wrong speed.

I lay back again and waited for Laura's signal . . . and waited.

'Harry,' I whispered. 'What do you think's happened to Laura?'

Harry just gave a snore in reply.

So it was up to me to find out. I climbed out of bed and went on to the landing, I saw Laura rightaway. She was standing under the landing light, which was always left on at night.

'Laura,' I whispered.

But she didn't turn around.

'Laura,' I called again, only this time much louder.

She gave a kind of jump, then whirled round, her eyes wide with terror.

I sprang forward. 'Laura, what is it? What's wrong?'

She didn't say anything, just started to shake.

I took hold of her hand. 'Laura, tell me what's happened?' She continued to shake. I was getting panicky now. 'Laura, speak to me.'

Instead, she just shook her head at me. It was then I remembered something.

The first time I'd met Laura was at infant school and she wouldn't speak to me. In fact, she wouldn't speak to anyone. Miss Bailey, our form teacher, said Laura was very sensitive and very shy and we mustn't force her to speak.

So, for some days Laura played with us and went to all our lessons without uttering one single word. It was very strange, especially as everyone else in the class talked non-stop.

In a way it made Laura quite

intriguing.

Then one day Miss Bailey wanted volunteers to be in a play about different birds and animals. And when Miss Bailey asked who wanted to be the nightingale, Laura's hand shot up. Everyone was astonished. But Miss Bailey picked Laura to be the nightingale. Later, when we started reading the play aloud Laura spoke for the first time—as the nightingale. She's gone on speaking ever since—until tonight.

'Laura, can't you speak?' I whispered. Laura shook her head, getting more and more agitated.

'That's all right,' I said, gently. 'Not talking is fine. Let's go to the kitchen. I'll make you a milkshake if you like.' Laura's face briefly lit up. She can't resist milkshakes.

So with my arm around her we slowly walked down to the kitchen. Then I set about making Laura a strawberry milkshake. I thought my mum or Roy might hear me and come charging downstairs demanding to know what I was doing. But no-one did.

I gave Laura the milkshake which she gulped down. 'Another one?' I asked. She nodded eagerly. While Laura was drinking her second strawberry milkshake I said, 'Do you remember what you said when you played the nightingale?'

At once Laura replied, 'I may look brown and ordinary but when I sing I have the most beautiful voice in the world.' Then she stopped and said in a kind of wonderment, 'My voice has come back. I thought I'd lost it again, I really did.'

'What happened, Laura?' I said, gently.

She started to shiver. 'I saw it,' she gasped.

'Saw what?'

'The ghost dog,' she cried, and all at once she was talking really quickly. 'It was waiting for me. I fell asleep and there it was. I saw its evil red eyes staring at me. And I called out; "What do you want?" Then I heard it say, "You, I've come back for you," and as it spoke blood poured out of its mouth.

It was the most horrible thing I'd ever seen in my life. And it was so close to me . . . I tried to scream.

'Only no sounds came out of my mouth. Instead, I jumped awake. But I could still sense the creature was somewhere near me. So I ran to the landing and stood under the light. Sometimes if I think about ghosts at home I'll go and stand under the landing light for a while and that always helps me, then I can go back to sleep. But this time it didn't help. Instead I kept seeing pictures in the light . . . pictures of that terrible dog with blood dripping out of his mouth.' She started to shake again.

'Can you see it now?' I asked.

'No, no,' she said. 'I think it's gone at last.' She turned to her milkshake and slurped up the remains of it. Her voice fell. 'I feel a bit silly now.'

'Well, don't,' I replied. 'I mean, tonight has been quite eerie, what with going to that old churchyard.'

'And hearing that dog howl,' said Laura.

'Yeah, that was a bit strange,' I agreed. 'So for a few minutes you forgot it wasn't real. But remember, there's no such thing as the ghost dog, actually.'

'Oh, I know,' said Laura.

'We just made it up, to scare Aaron.'

'And we did scare Aaron, didn't we?' Laura smiled. 'The way he dropped that stone as if it had just bitten him . . .' Then she added, 'You won't tell anyone about tonight, will you?'

'Of course not,' I replied. 'It's our secret for ever.'

'Thanks, Dan.'

'That's OK. After all, you never told about the time *The Wizard of Oz* scared me. Remember?'

'Oh, yes,' cried Laura. 'It was the trees you didn't like, wasn't it?'

'That's right. And the way they kept moving about and talking . . . that really gave me the creeps.' I shook my head. 'Imagine being scared by *The Wizard of Oz*, that's deeply shaming, but you never gave my secret away—so one good turn deserves another.'

We crept upstairs, whispering together. But when we reached Laura's room, she said, 'Wait there a moment, will you, Dan?' And when she returned she was holding the stone in her hand. 'Would you mind keeping this for the

65

rest of the night, please?' she asked.

'No, sure. Of course not,' I said, as confidently as I could. Inside my bedroom Aaron and Harry were both snoring. I put the stone on my little cabinet then I climbed into bed.

'It's just a stone,' I kept saying to myself. But still, it took me ages to get to sleep. I couldn't help thinking about that ghost dog too.

The next thing I knew Mum was drawing the curtains and asking us how we'd all slept. I blinked and smiled. Not even the whisper of a dream about the ghost dog. I felt ashamed of myself for even thinking such a thing.

'All right lads, rise and shine,' said Mum as she opened the bedroom window wide. 'That's what this room needs, fresh air . . . breakfast in ten minutes.'

At once, Aaron rushed off to the bathroom.

'He'll be in there for ages now,' I moaned to Harry.

But Harry just muttered: 'Why is everyone up so early?' and fell asleep again. In the end I left Harry sleeping while I got dressed.

As I came out of the bathroom I bumped into Laura. She looked very pale and tired. 'How are you?' I asked.

'I'm OK,' said Laura quietly. Then her voice rose. 'Don't tell anyone about last night, will you?'

'Of course not, I promised.'

'Not even Harry?'

'OK, not even Harry.'

She gave a faint smile. 'Thanks, Dan . . . I'm ashamed. That horrible dream seems so silly now.' She shivered. 'Yet

67

last night . . .'

'You just got a bit carried away,' I interrupted. 'You do that sometimes. What about that play where you had to cry at the end, and then you couldn't stop crying?'

'Yes, I remember, I do get carried away.' That thought seemed to reassure her. 'And that's what happened to me last night.' Laura gave another half-smile.

My bedroom door burst open, and there was Harry standing in his pyjamas. His hair was all sticking up at the back and he was yawning and looked so sleepy that Laura and I both burst out laughing.

'I could sleep for another week,' he muttered. Then he grinned. 'It was a brilliant crack with Aaron last night, wasn't it? Especially the moment when he was so scared he dropped the stone.' He started to laugh and we joined in, Laura rather uneasily.

'Do you suppose we gave Aaron any nightmares?' asked Harry. Laura half-turned away; a deep red blush was creeping up her neck.

'I'm sure we did,' I replied.

Harry gave another triumphant grin before falling into the bathroom.

After breakfast I went into town with Laura and Harry. We hung around the sports shop where we met up with mates from school. Then we went ice-skating. By the evening, though, I was dead tired, so I just crashed out on the sofa watching some videos Roy had bought. Suddenly, from upstairs we heard, 'Mummy, can I have a drink please?'

'Oh, Carrie, I thought you were asleep hours ago,' cried Mum. 'All right, I won't be a minute.'

As Mum left, Roy said, 'OK boys,

69

bedtime for you two, I think.'

I didn't know if I liked Roy giving me orders. That was Mum's job, not his. Still, Aaron and I trooped upstairs in silence; we'd hardly spoken to each other all day. Aaron charged into the bathroom. It was good to have my bedroom to myself for a few minutes.

I picked up the stone from last night. I was going to put it in the box by my wardrobe where I kept all my junk. But I took one last look at it. It fascinated me. It was so jagged and heavy; it was a bit like one of those axes cavemen used. Maybe it had been. Stones can be thousands of years old. I was just thinking about this when I heard a loud sighing behind me.

Aaron was glaring at me.

'What's the matter with you?' I asked.

Aaron shook his head. 'You're pathetic.'

'What are you going on about?' I demanded.

'You and that stone, you think you're so funny, don't you.'

'I was just looking at it,' I began.

70

'Yeah, yeah, I know what you were doing. That stone, you couldn't just have got rid of it like any normal person, could you? No, you've got to keep it here.'

'What's it to you, anyway?' I said. 'Unless this stone scares you.'

'Oh yeah, I mean, it's such a scary stone, isn't it?' jeered Aaron.

'Well, you were afraid to take it home,' I taunted.

'No, I wasn't.'

'Yes, you were,' I cried. 'Your hand was shaking when you held that stone.'

'Yeah, it was shaking with laughter.'

'You liar,' I cried.

Aaron's voice began to rise. 'Do you think I believed that stupid story you told me?'

'You believed every word and you dropped that stone because you were scared out of your wits.'

'I was not.' Aaron was practically screaming at me now.

'Scared out of your wits,' I repeated.

My bedroom door flew open and Mum and Roy were standing there.

'We were just discussing something,' I mumbled.

'Well, you were making far too much noise,' began Mum. Then all at once

Roy exploded beside her. 'I don't know what's going on in here. You've got this nice big room with plenty of space for two people. So what's the big problem . . . WHAT IS THE PROBLEM?' Roy stopped for breath. His mouth had gone down at the corners and his eyes were bulging: at me. Roy had obviously decided I was the main culprit here.

'I think you both behaved badly,' cut in Mum, perhaps to stop Roy going on with his very biased view of events, 'and I think the sooner you both get to sleep the better.' She half-pushed Roy out of the bedroom. He looked as if he had a bit more to say: all against me, no doubt.

I lay in my bunk, stunned. I'd quite liked Roy before. But tonight, he'd shown himself in his true colours. Whatever happened, it would always be me in the wrong, never his precious son.

I glared down at Aaron. 'Been crying to your daddy about me, haven't you?'

'I wouldn't waste a second talking about you,' snapped Aaron.

I was shaking with anger now. I

didn't want Aaron in my house, in my bedroom. He was just ruining everything. In the end I was shaking so much I had to get up. I let Rocky out. He kept on wanting to be stroked, so I just sat on the floor, stroking him and whispering, 'One day we'll have this room to ourselves again.' After a while I began to feel sleepy so I put Rocky in his cage and got back into bed again.

It still took me ages to get off to sleep, though. I was tossing and turning until finally I was walking somewhere. There was a heavy, grey mist so I couldn't see where I was going. I just knew the ground felt soft and squelchy: as if it were trying to drag me down into it. And the air was so cold and stale it was making me cough.

Where was I? I didn't like this place. I wanted to be away from here. And then I caught a glimpse of something, the tree which was bent double. Here it was, looking more sad and pathetic than ever. And beside it were all the stones. The stones which were supposed to mark the dog's grave.

I must be back in the old churchyard.

Only I couldn't make out anything else. I coughed again. The mist seemed to be getting into my lungs.

Then from out of nowhere came this howling noise. The same howling we'd heard that night at the churchyard. Only this time it sounded much louder. I peered around. I was being watched. Just a few feet away from me were a pair of eyes: bright, burning red eyes that looked right through me. I could feel my heart beating in my mouth, I was too terrified to move. At first.

Suddenly, I was running, as fast as I could. But it was very hard to run on this soft mud. It was like trying to run in quicksand. And then I sensed hot breath on my neck. It was right behind me. It'll get me, I must run faster . . . faster . . . I jumped awake, gasping for breath, and my heart was still pounding furiously.

'Calm down. It's over,' I told myself. Through the curtains I could see a faint, grey light. It was still very early. I should go back to sleep. But I daren't. For I knew what would be waiting for me.

So instead, I just lay there hour after hour, envying Aaron his calm, restful sleep. I heard the clatter and jangle of the paper boy slamming the Sunday papers through the letterbox, and then the phone started to ring, loudly, urgently.

My mum had a phone in her room, so I heard her say, in a very sleepy voice, '784612.' And then: 'Well, I'll see if he's awake. It is Sunday morning, you know.' Then Mum appeared in my doorway. 'Dan, are you awake?'

'Yes, I'm awake,' I said. I'd been awake half the night.

'It's Laura on the phone for you. She

sounds quite upset. Do you want to take it in the kitchen?'

I shot downstairs to the kitchen.

'Hi, Laura.'

'I didn't wake you up, did I?'

'No, not at all. What's up?'

She was speaking very slowly: 'Dan, it came back last night. That ghost dog. I saw it, and it scared me so much.' There was a pause before she whispered, 'Dan, what am I going to do?'

'Don't worry,' I said. 'I saw it last night too.'

'You did,' she exclaimed.

'So you're not the only one,' I said. 'And listen, we're going to sort this out. I'll be round your house rightaway.'

CHAPTER FIVE

Laura was waiting outside her house for me.

'I came as fast as I could,' I gasped. And although we don't normally do anything corny, I gave her hand a squeeze.

Her mum welcomed me enthusiastically. 'Come to cheer Laura up, have you? Splendid. She had a bad nightmare last night. Tea and toast for both of you?' We both nodded eagerly.

Laura whispered, 'Mum just thinks I had a nightmare. She's been really nice to me. So's Dad. She doesn't know anything about the ghost dog.'

Over tea and toast we compared our nightmares. They were pretty similar. Only Laura was in a wood when she saw the ghost dog, not in the churchyard.

'I think it would be even worse seeing it in that old churchyard,' said Laura.

'It was,' I agreed. 'All the ground was soggy and you could hardly run in it . . . still, it must have been pretty scary in the wood.'

'I kept running into the branches of trees,' said Laura, 'and twice I fell over.

79

When I woke up I really thought I'd sprained my ankle, just like you did at your party.'

Laura's mum appeared again. 'Phone for you, Laura,' she said.

Laura rushed off and was gone some time. When she came back, she said, 'You'll never guess who that was?'

'Father Christmas.'

'No, Harry.'

'I was close, then. So what did old Harry want?'

'He says he saw it too . . . the ghost dog.'

I gazed at her, stunned. 'Are you sure he wasn't messing about?'

Laura shook her head. 'He sounded really worked up. He said he'd tried ringing you but your mum told him you were here. He's coming over too.'

And a few minutes later there was a surprisingly serious Harry, also having tea and toast. He had seen the ghost dog outside his house. It was getting dark and he was about to draw the curtains when he heard a terrible howling noise. And then he saw this huge dog banging its head against the glass, struggling to get in. He was absolutely terrified and woke himself up, yelling loudly.

I shook my head in astonishment. So the ghost dog had appeared in all three of our dreams last night. 'Well, you certainly can't say this dog is lazy. He keeps busy, doesn't he?' I said.

Laura and Harry managed small smiles. 'How long do you think this will go on?' asked Harry. 'Will he turn up again tonight?'

'I don't think so,' I said. 'I'm sure it's over now. I mean, look, what we've got to remember is, the ghost dog isn't real. I made it all up.'

'Are you sure?' asked Harry, suddenly. 'Where did that story about the dog and his grave come from?'

I shrugged my shoulders. 'My imagination.'

'But you thought you saw something when you switched the hall light off to play *Murder in the Dark*,' said Laura.

'A dog, wasn't it?' murmured Harry.

All of a sudden they were both staring intently at me.

'All right,' I said. 'I might have seen

something then, although that was probably just imagination too. And everything else certainly was. There's no such thing as the ghost dog.'

Harry and Laura looked at me doubtfully. Then Harry said, quietly, 'I think we should take the stone back.'

'Why?' I exclaimed.

'The dog said, if anyone took so much as one stone away from his grave he would haunt them for ever,' said Harry, in the same quiet tone.

'Now you're being really stupid,' I cried. 'We made that curse up. In fact, you made that part up, Harry.'

'Did I?' Harry sounded puzzled.

'Yes, don't you remember Aaron said my story was a load of old rubbish, so to try and scare him you added the bit about the stone.'

'But it wouldn't do any harm to take the stone back,' began Laura.

'Yes, it would,' I interrupted. 'That stone is nothing. I'd feel really stupid taking it back. It would be like we'd ended up fooling ourselves.'

'Look, Dan,' said Harry. 'That dream really freaked me out last night.

And I don't want to see that ghost dog again. He's too noisy for a start, howling and head-banging. All the neighbours are complaining . . .' Then he added, almost pleadingly, 'If you don't want to go, give the stone to Laura and me. We'll take it back.'

'That stone is staying in my bedroom,' I said. 'You and Laura are just being daft.'

Laura's mum appeared to clear away. 'More tea, anyone?'

'We couldn't eat another thing,' I replied.

Laura's mum smiled, then she said, 'Laura's lucky to have friends like you, rushing round to cheer her up. Nightmares can be so powerful, can't they? Poor Laura couldn't stop shaking when she woke up.'

I looked across at Laura's pale face. Her eyes looked very large this morning. I couldn't help feeling a stab of sympathy for her. And although all three of us had made the story up, I'd started it, hadn't I? I was the most to blame.

So after Laura's mum had gone, I

said, 'OK, if you really want to take the stone back, we will.'

'Dan, put it there,' said Harry, shaking my hand.

'Can we do it today?' asked Laura.

So after lunch I went up to my room and took the stone out of my wardrobe. As I stared at it I thought I could make out bits of faces: a nose here, an eye there. 'This stone's certainly got charisma,' I said to myself. But to be honest, I wasn't altogether sorry to be getting rid of it.

It was a damp, drizzly afternoon when the three of us set off. By the time we reached the churchyard it was

already quite dark. But then this seemed the kind of place where it was always grey and gloomy. We found the old bent tree easily. It looked exactly as it had in my nightmare. My heart started to thump.

The clock in the church tower chimed loudly above us. We all stared at the church for a moment.

'They say you can see shapes in the church windows,' said Laura. 'They're supposed to be angels watching us.'

'Well, we need all the help we can get,' I said briskly.

'Maybe the angels are cross with us,' said Laura.

'What are you rabbiting on about?' I asked.

'Well, we were a bit nasty to Aaron last night, weren't we?' said Laura. 'Me, included,' she added hastily.

'*We* were nasty!' I exclaimed. 'What about him, sneering at us and . . . ?'

'Oh, I know he deserved it,' interrupted Laura.

'And how would you like to have Aaron in your bedroom every night?' I ranted on.

'I don't think he'd be allowed in Laura's bedroom every night,' said Harry, trying to make a joke of it all. 'And look, can we just get this over with?'

'OK then,' I said, taking the stone from my pocket.

'Do you think we ought to say something?' asked Laura.

'What do you suggest? Goodbye, Mr Stone, have a nice life?' I replied.

'There's no need to be sarky,' she said, quietly. 'I just think we should say we're sorry for disturbing it.'

'Well, you can say that, I'm not,' I said, handing her the stone.

It was exactly then a dog started to bark. I must admit it gave us all a start and Laura nearly dropped the stone with shock. 'Dogs are always barking, aren't they?' she gasped.

'That's right, it's just here we notice it more,' I said.

The rain was starting to come down really heavily now and it was becoming colder, too. That probably explains why we'd all started shivering.

'We're so sorry for disturbing you,'

86

said Laura, in a voice so low I could hardly hear her. 'We should never have done it. But we've brought you back, so please leave us in peace now.'

'I've heard it all now,' I muttered, 'grovelling to a stone.'

Laura continued to look serious as she very gently lowered the stone on to the ground. Part of me wanted to laugh. But another part of me felt uneasy. I really didn't like this place. I gave a kind of half-shiver, then said, 'It's funny, really, we invent this story about the stone, and the ghost dog, to scare Aaron and he's the only one who's not here, getting soaked to the skin.'

Harry gave a small smile. 'That trick back-fired on us, all right. Still, it's all over now, so come on, let's get out of here.'

We walked quickly away, practically sprinting up Church Walk. It was only when we were back in the village High Street that we started to slow down. 'I've just remembered,' I cried. 'We've got to go back. I've forgotten something.'

'What?' cried Laura.

'I was going to take another stone away, just as a souvenir.'

'Yeah, yeah, yeah,' grinned Harry. 'We do believe you.' And then all three of us were laughing with relief. 'I'll tell you something for nothing,' said Harry. 'I never want to go back to that place again.'

'I wouldn't go if you paid me,' declared Laura.

'Well, I might, if you paid me,' I said. But then I added, 'No, I never want to go back there again either.'

'So where shall we go?' asked Harry.

'How about walking into town? McDonald's will be open,' said Laura.

Inside McDonald's we all pigged out on Big Macs, chips and chocolate milkshakes. Then Harry ordered some chicken nuggets.

'You're hungry,' said Laura.

'Not really,' replied Harry. 'Just very relieved.'

I knew exactly what he meant.

When I got home, Mum was waiting for me.

'Can I have a quick word?'

'You can have a long word, if you like,' I said.

'It's about Aaron,' began Mum. Inside I groaned. I should have guessed. 'Roy's going away in a few minutes,' she went on, 'and I think Aaron's quite upset about that. He's hardly eaten a thing all day.'

'Oh, no, what a tragedy,' I said, with undisguised sarcasm.

'Now, don't be like that,' said Mum. 'You can be such a thoughtful boy when you like. Be helpful to Aaron . . . for my sake, please.'

Just then Roy and Aaron appeared. Roy was all smiles, patting me on the head and even giving me a small present. But his cover had been blown. I knew that he'd always see everything just from Aaron's point of view.

Roy gave Mum a hug goodbye, and I heard him whispering to her, 'Look, we really can work this out, you know.' I wondered what he meant by that, and hoped it wasn't anything to do with me. I bet it was. Then Roy gave Aaron a punch and told him to 'get involved', shook hands with me, and kissed the top of Carrie's head.

'That tickled,' she muttered.

Later, Mum was saying to Aaron, 'He'll be back before you know it. The weeks will just fly by.' Aaron didn't really reply and his face was expressionless, dead. It was hard to know if he was upset or not.

I went to my bedroom quite early that night. Aaron was already there, lying in his bunk reading a book. Neither of us spoke. There was a tense, uncomfortable silence. Once or twice I did try and say something, just to break the awful atmosphere. But everything I thought of sounded silly and I didn't want to say anything which Aaron could sneer at. So in the end I just chatted to Rocky.

Then I clambered up into bed. I nearly called out, 'Night,' but lost my nerve. Instead, I tried to get to sleep. I expected to lie awake for hours, but instead I fell asleep almost at once, and found myself in a place where it was dark and misty, and wet. Even before I saw the old bent tree, I knew where I was.

The mist had thickened tonight wrapping itself around everything, except . . . Nothing could hold this creature back. There it was, looming over me: bigger than ever. Only tonight, its massive jaws were half-open. I always hate it when you can see a dog's sharp teeth. Now I could make out something else. Blood dripping from its mouth. The blood of one of its other victims. Like Laura or Harry. And once it had got the taste for humans . . .

Suddenly, it lunged forward and I let out such a terrible scream I woke myself up. Waves of sweat were rolling off me. I pushed the covers off. I still felt as if I were burning up, while shivers were running up and down my back.

It was so close tonight. If I hadn't woken up then, that dog would have got me for sure. Maybe it had got Laura or Harry. Should I ring and find out? No, their parents would go mad.

What I didn't understand was: we'd taken the stone back. The dog should leave us alone now. But then I remembered the original curse: the dog said, if anyone took so much as one stone away from his grave he would haunt them for ever. There was nothing about what the dog would do if you took the stone back.

Maybe, once we'd released the dog into our dreams, that was it. There was no letting go of it after that. Every night now for the rest of our lives Laura, Harry and I would see that dog, until . . . another part of the story flashed into my head. The dog went on haunting the boy until the boy was found dead with a look of such terror on his face . . . After that I had to get out of bed and start pacing around my

room. Why had I made up such a stupid story? For now the story was in our heads and we couldn't get rid of it. The dog could be attacking Laura or Harry now.

And it was mostly my fault.

I climbed back into bed. Below me Aaron was fast asleep, but making those funny breathing noises. I drifted off to sleep but I kept thinking I saw the ghost dog and jumping awake.

At breakfast time I staggered downstairs. I gave Rocky some Marmite on toast which he gobbled down. But I wasn't at all hungry and neither, strangely enough, was Aaron. Mum tut-tutted in annoyance. 'Breakfast is the most important meal of the day, you know. What's the matter with you both?'

'Just not hungry, Mum,' I said weakly. Outside, Harry and Laura were waiting for me. I was actually relieved to see them. I'd had this horrible vision of them being so badly mauled by the dog that they couldn't escape and had to stay in that nightmare. But as soon as I saw their pale, tense faces, I knew they'd been visited by the ghost dog too.

'I was in the wood and this thing jumped out of the bushes at me,' cried Laura.

'It nearly got in the house,' said Harry. 'I saw this dark shadow scraping at the door so hard. Next time . . .'

'What are we going to do?' cried Laura. She and Harry were looking at me expectantly.

And right then it came to me. Yes, of course, why hadn't I thought of that before?

'I've got an idea,' I said.

CHAPTER SIX

That evening Harry, Laura and me went back to the hut. It was my idea.

'So, come on,' said Harry to me, 'you can tell us now. Why have you got us to come back here?'

I leaned forward. 'This is the place where we created the ghost dog . . .'

'So,' interrupted Harry.

'So, this seems the ideal place to tame it.'

'Tame it?' echoed Laura.

'That's right,' I said. 'Tonight we're going to tame the ghost dog by telling funny stories about it. Then the next

95

time we see it we'll just burst out laughing and it won't be able to scare us any more.' Laura and Harry looked at me doubtfully. 'Look,' I exclaimed, 'we made the dog spooky, so we can make it . . .' I searched for the right word, 'unspooky.' Laura and Harry looked at me doubtfully. I pressed on. 'First of all we need to give it a stupid name, like, The Mutt.'

'Or Goofy,' cried Laura.

'Or what about Spurs,' said Harry. 'That's a really stupid name, especially for a football team.' Both he and Laura were Manchester United supporters.

'Here, watch it,' I said, 'or we'll be calling it Man United, for sure.'

'How about Bonzo or Gonzo,' said Laura.

'Gonzo,' I repeated. 'That's a really silly name for a dog. Come on, Gonzo, walkies.' I started to laugh. 'So tonight when you see the dog, or if you do,' I added hastily, seeing Laura's anxious face, 'call out, Gonzo, here Gonzo.'

'And you can keep calling out Gonzo as it pulls your leg off,' said Harry.

'Oh come on, give this a chance,' I

replied. 'Now, what else would make this dog look really silly?'

'A pink ribbon,' suggested Laura.

'Brilliant,' I cried. 'I can see it now, Gonzo in a pink ribbon.'

'And one of those silly dog coats as well,' said Laura.

'Why not?' I agreed. 'This dog is going to look so daft tonight.'

'How about if it's wearing glasses?' asked Harry.

'I don't know,' said Laura. 'That might make his red eyes even bigger.'

'Tinted glasses, then,' suggested Harry.

'I think we should leave the glasses, but it should definitely have one of those high-pitched barks,' I said.

'And whenever you hum it starts dancing,' cried Laura.

'Now that would be a real crack,' I laughed.

'But tonight, will it . . .?' began Laura, doubtfully.

'Gonzo will do all of these daft things because it's our dog. We made it. But we've got to keep seeing Gonzo doing things like that.'

At once all three of us started concentrating hard on Gonzo with his pink ribbon and dog coat, and dancing away to any tune we hummed.

'When I see that dog tonight,' said Harry, 'I'm just going to laugh and laugh and laugh.'

'What will happen to Gonzo when we laugh at it?' asked Laura.

'He will get smaller,' I replied, 'until finally he will shrink away to nothing.'

'I've got this picture in my head now,' said Laura, 'of first of all its body disappearing, then its legs, and finally there's just this head floating around, until that starts to fade away too.'

'I don't care how it disappears,' said Harry, 'just provided it does—and it never comes back again either.'

'Well, if it does try to return we just laugh at it again, then it will soon go. And remember, call out Gonzo when you see it,' I said.

'Gonzo,' Harry grinned. 'You could almost feel sorry for a dog with a name like that. Almost.'

We left the hut in an optimistic, cheerful mood. But back in my house, I just felt scared again. What if my idea didn't work?

'Time for bed,' called Mum.

'OK,' I replied. But I didn't move. The phone rang. It was Laura. 'I'm just ringing up for a chat and a bit of confidence,' she whispered.

Talking to Laura made me feel certain again. My plan would work.

Mum appeared. I thought she was going to tell me off for not being in bed. Instead, she asked, 'Did you have a good time?' She was smiling, sort of.

'Yeah, great.'

'Were you telling ghost stories

again?' she asked.

'Something like that. Only funnier ones.'

'Aaron's still not eating properly,' she said, suddenly. 'But every time I say anything he tells me he's just not hungry.' Now Mum was looking to me for a bit of confidence. She did that sometimes, especially when she was worried about Carrie.

'He's just missing Roy,' I said. 'When's Roy back from America, then?'

Mum's face grew even tenser. 'I really don't know,' she said. Then she added: 'If Aaron does try and talk to you, don't . . . well, give him a chance.'

'I'm the last person he'd talk to. He'd be more likely to talk to Carrie than me.'

Mum gave another sigh and disappeared. She seemed really wound up tonight.

Upstairs, Aaron was asleep already. After saying 'Goodnight' to Rocky I got into bed too. My eyes burned with tiredness. I closed them. I tried to picture Gonzo wearing a pink ribbon, a

100

dog coat and glasses . . . no, not glasses. Not even tinted ones . . . When I opened my eyes again I saw it rightaway, crouched in the darkness.

I peered through the mist. Yes, it was wearing a pink ribbon all right. And a dog coat.

My plan was working.

That made me a little more confident. 'Gonzo,' I whispered. 'Gonzo.'

All at once those red eyes were beamed right at me. Some of my confidence oozed away again. We should have changed the dog's eyes: made them smaller. I suppose it was too late now.

And then it gave this very low snarl.

'That's not how you bark, you've got a high-pitched bark,' I cried.

At once the dog started making this very shrill yelping sound. It sounded like someone playing the same high note over and over again. It set my teeth on edge. 'No, stop that.' The dog obeyed instantly. But then I heard it snarling again. I was becoming confused now. And scared.

I remembered this dog danced if you hummed a tune. Now that sight would make it look totally ridiculous. I hummed the first few bars of the theme tune to *Neighbours*. That was enough. The dog was on its feet. I gulped. It looked bigger than ever.

'Now, come on, dance,' I cried. The dog lumbered to its feet and made that low, snarling noise in its throat again.

'Dance,' I squeaked.

Instead the dog took a giant step towards me. My knees started knocking together and then I totally lost my bottle and ran for it. Only I didn't get very far. I ran straight into this tree and fell flat on my face. I lay there, floundering about in the mud, and sensed this shadow towering over me.

I slammed shut my eyes. At least I didn't have to see it. But I could still hear it breathing really heavily. I could smell its stale, rotting breath too. It must be very close to me. The smell was making me heave.

And then I felt sharp teeth cutting into my left leg. The pain was excruciating. 'NO, NO, NO, NO.'

I opened my eyes. But it was no good. I couldn't see anything but darkness now. What had happened to me? I was sick with fear until slowly it dawned on me, I had my hand clamped over my face.

I took my hand away and gazed around at my bedroom. I was back. But relief quickly turned to disappointment. I'd thought by making fun of the dog I could make it disappear. But it hadn't worked. Why? Because I was still scared of it, that's why. And the dog knew that. Now every night it would be waiting for me, and there would be no holding it back. It would . . .

It was then I heard a noise which made my whole body freeze. Something was scratching at the wall behind me. Something was trying to get in.

It was the ghost dog. It has followed me out of my dream. And now it was scratching its way into my bedroom— just like in the story I'd told. It had got a taste of my flesh and now it wants more.

I heard it again, louder this time: scratching wildly, fiercely. Nothing was going to stop it getting through. I wanted to bury my head under the sheets, pretend I hadn't heard anything, go to sleep. Only, I didn't dare do that because it would be waiting for me there, too.

So I didn't do anything. I couldn't. My whole body had gone numb. I just lay there, frozen to the spot until finally I thought, this must still be a dream, I haven't woken up. I rubbed my eyes.

The scratching went on. Then I rubbed my eyes really hard. If anything, the noise became even louder.

So I must be awake, which means . . . which means, any second now that dog will come tearing into my bedroom. And tomorrow morning my mum will draw back the curtains and see me lying there, my face frozen for ever in a look of such terror she'll never be able to forget it.

I should try and escape, leg it downstairs. But what's the point? It'll find me there too. There's no escaping the ghost dog. I closed my eyes, then almost at once they flew open again. Someone was calling my name. 'Daniel, Daniel,' the voice called, loudly, urgently. There was a pause for a moment before the voice cried, 'Daniel, please help me.' It was then I realized who was calling me.

It was Aaron.

CHAPTER SEVEN

I climbed out of bed and switched on the light, and stood for a second under the bedroom light, just as Laura does when she's scared, and this helped to calm me down a bit.

That scratching noise had really got me worked up. Now, with the light on, it sounded fainter and less scary. Perhaps it was just a bird or something.

Then I went over to Aaron. 'Why have you been calling me?' I demanded. The only reply from Aaron was a heavy, rhythmic, breathing noise. He must have called my name out in his sleep. How strange.

Then I watched Aaron raise his right hand and start scratching the wall behind him. So it was he who'd been scaring me half to death. For a second I was relieved, then I was mad. Trust Aaron to be the cause of the scratching noise. But then he caused all the hassle in my life. It was Aaron's fault we made up that story about the ghost dog. He was to blame for everything. I didn't really believe that, but it was good to dump all the blame on to someone else.

I glared down at Aaron just as he opened his eyes. He stared up at me, totally bewildered. 'What do you want?'

'You called me,' I replied shortly.

'I did what?' he asked, in that superior tone of his, which I hated so much.

'Just forget it,' I snapped. 'But you woke me up calling my name and scratching at the wall.' Aaron noticed he still had his right hand raised. He hastily lowered it. 'But if you want to pretend you didn't call me, then that's fine.' I made as if to climb back into bed.

That's when Aaron said, 'Yes, I did call you.' He whispered this as if he were confessing to some terrible crime.

'Make your mind up, won't you,' I snapped. But I was more embarrassed than angry. I hovered awkwardly in front of him. 'Why did you call me?' And my voice came out like a croak. It felt very strange talking to Aaron.

Aaron didn't reply at first. Then when he did speak he swallowed his words as if he couldn't hold them in his mouth very easily. 'I guess I needed your help.'

'You needed my help,' I repeated incredulously.

'I've needed your help for some days, actually, but I didn't tell you before because . . .' He shrugged his shoulders. 'But what does that matter now?' He half-looked at me. 'All right, you win.'

I shook my head. 'I don't understand.'

Aaron's voice started to rise. 'The dog you told me about to try and scare me, well you succeeded all right. Every night I see it and it terrifies the life out of me all right.' He was clenching his hands into fists as he went on. 'That dog, that monster has really got to me. I can't stop thinking about it. Even during the day it's like this giant shadow . . . I've even lost my appetite, which I thought would never happen.' He clenched his fists even tighter and stared down at them. 'So, like I said, you win, OK.'

'Where do you see this dog?' I asked.

'Same place every night, in the old churchyard that we went to.'

I started. So he'd seen the ghost dog in exactly the same place as I had.

'Tonight,' said Aaron, 'the dog had this pink ribbon on and he was wearing a kind of coat.'

That stunned me.

'But somehow,' went on Aaron, 'that just made it more weird and scary.'

'The story about the dog,' I said, slowly, 'it's not really true. I made it up to scare you.'

'Oh I guessed that,' replied Aaron at once. 'Still, I've got to admit, it scared me all right.'

I edged closer to Aaron: 'We scared ourselves too,' I admitted. 'Harry and Laura see the dog every night.' I stared down at his blue bed cover. 'And so do I.'

'You see it,' he gasped.

'Lucky me, huh,' I smiled grimly. Then staring even more intently at the blue bed cover, I said, 'Since you moved in here it's all been a bit of a disaster, hasn't it?'

'A total disaster,' agreed Aaron. 'But I know I did it all wrong. You see, I didn't want to move away from my old school, I had some brilliant mates there. But since my mum died, we're always on the move. Dad says he's got itchy feet and now he's jetting off to America. But I want to . . . I hate all this moving about.'

Then speaking all in a rush, he went on, 'That Spiderman costume, I should never have worn that to your party. It was far too flash. But Dad would have been offended if I hadn't and he sulks, you know. Wouldn't speak to me for three days once. So I was stuck. Still, I can't blame people for hating me that night. Although most of them hated me long before that . . .' His voice rose. 'You turned everyone against me, didn't you?'

I could feel myself turning bright red. 'I thought you were trying to steal my friends,' I muttered. Yet, even as I said them, the words sounded so feeble and little kiddish: the sort of thing Carrie might say.

'I wasn't trying to steal your friends,' said Aaron.

'I know,' I replied.

'But I don't blame you,' went on Aaron. 'You've got to protect yourself. That's what we were both doing.'

Suddenly I stopped examining the bed cover and looked straight at Aaron. And he looked straight at me.

'Yeah, you've got to protect yourself,' I repeated quickly. 'But I'm sorry about . . . things.'

Aaron seemed slightly taken aback by this apology. And he let my sentence hang in the air for a moment. Finally, he asked, 'Do you think you can get rid of this dog?' He gave a confiding smile. 'I'm getting a bit desperate here.'

'I made the dog, so I should be able to get rid of it. Only, somehow I always end up running away from it.'

'I can see why,' said Aaron.

I shook my head. 'No, I shouldn't be running away from a dog I made up. That would be like an author being scared of one of his characters. Why, an author can just wipe out a character any time he likes. And so, that means . . . that means I can do it, too. Just wipe the dog out.' And as I said these words I could feel this tremendous power building up inside me. I'd had the same feeling when I made up the story of the ghost dog.

'Up to now,' I said, 'I've been really halfhearted and weedy, running away from the dog every time it so much as growled. But not any more . . . this time I'm going right up to it and face it and . . . well, it's up to me, isn't it.' And as I said these words I felt quite brave and heroic as if I were riding into battle to save others. 'Now, what's the time?'

'Just gone four,' said Aaron.

'Right, well there's still time to meet my monster, eyeball to eyeball.'

Aaron stared at me, grinning: 'What can I say, but good luck . . . and you're a mighty warrior.'

I grinned back. 'I'll probably lose all

my courage before I go to sleep,' I said.

'No, you won't, Dan,' said Aaron, firmly. 'By the way, I probably won't go to sleep straightaway, so is it all right if I play with Rocky for a while?'

I felt a flash of irritation. Rocky was my pet, not his. But then I thought: where's the harm in sharing Rocky? 'Yeah, sure, Rocky likes company,' I said. I closed my eyes; straightaway I could hear Aaron whispering to Rocky. I lay listening for a while and then I was faraway from them . . . faraway.

It felt different there this time. Perhaps because the wind was blowing really fiercely and the trees were shaking and sighing to themselves. It was as if they knew something was about to happen.

My heart began to beat furiously. This time, I couldn't fail.

'Gonzo, where are you?' I called. And then I saw it, just a few feet away from me. Or rather I saw those red eyes. The rest of it was, as usual, partly camouflaged by the thick grey mist.

Then, all at once the dog let out the most terrible howl I'd ever heard. Once that would have been enough to make me run for my life. And I'll admit, my legs wobbled more than a bit. But I told myself, I made this dog, I had the power.

I edged forward. The dog's eyes never left me. But I kept moving nearer to it. I'd told Aaron I'd face this dog eyeball to eyeball and that was what I was going to do.

Finally, I was just inches away from the dog. It was still wearing that pink ribbon and dog coat. But they just looked like a cheap joke now.

'That ribbon and coat should disappear,' I said. And to my total amazement, they did. They vanished rightaway.

Then I heard a voice say, 'Thank you, at least, for that, now go away before I bite you.'

The dog's voice was low and weary, like a very tired old man.

'I'm not going away. And you won't bite me,' I said.

As if in reply, the dog bared his teeth. I almost cried out, but nothing could stop me moving forward now. Suddenly my legs were as light as air. I wasn't so much walking as gliding.

And the nearer I got to those glowing, red eyes, the smaller they seemed.

Finally, I was right in front of the ghost dog. We were eyeball to eyeball as I'd promised Aaron. It was then the wind gave a deafening shriek and the mist started to shake as if it were being pulled away. And that's exactly what happened. The mist flew right into my face and then was swept away.

For the first time the ghost dog wasn't camouflaged by the mist. I could see it really clearly.

And what I saw made me cry out

with horror.

For the dog was nothing but skin and bone. I could even make out its rib cage. And it had little lumps all over its body: they were bruises, some of which were still bleeding.

'Who did this to you?' I cried.

'Humans, who else?' said the dog. 'If my owner was feeling angry about something he'd throw me against the wall, made him feel better somehow.'

I started to shiver. This poor dog was in a terrible state. Why hadn't I noticed it before?

The least I could do was bathe the dog's wounds. But I needed a bowl of water and a sponge for that. I pictured them in my head and, rightaway, there was a bowl of water and a sponge beside me. 'I'm going to bathe your wounds,' I said.

The dog made as if to resist and tried to get to its feet, but it couldn't. It fell back to the ground again.

'You can hardly move,' I said. 'Yet, every night you chased after me.'

The dog shook its head. 'All I can do are a few tricks like this,' and it lifted

118

back its head and gave this chilling howl which, even now, started my heart beating furiously. 'I'm pretty good at snarling too and showing my teeth. I leave the rest to your imagination.'

I felt rather foolish now. 'So each night I've been running away from nothing. We all have.'

The dog nodded. 'And very funny you looked too, running round and round in a circle every night.'

'What about the time I saw you at my Halloween party, was that just imagination too?'

'Just imagination,' repeated the dog. 'Don't you know, nothing's stronger than imagination. Nothing.'

'But why did you let us go on scaring ourselves?'

'You have to protect yourself,' replied the dog.

'That's just what Aaron said,' I murmured, but I don't think the dog heard me, for it went on, 'Human beings have caused me so much pain, you know. How was I to know you were any different?'

'Let me at least bathe your wounds

now,' I said, gently.

'You're wasting your time,' said the dog, but it didn't try and stop me.

'You must be in terrible pain,' I said.

The dog didn't answer this either, it just said, 'By the way, my name's not Gonzo, thank goodness.' It shuddered. 'It's Billy.'

'Billy, that's a good name,' I said.

'I know,' replied the dog, proudly.

When I'd finished I said, 'I expect you're hungry.'

'Not any more,' said the dog. 'I stopped being hungry a long time ago. All I want is for someone to make me a grave.'

I gave a little shiver. 'If that's what you want I'll do that,' I said. 'But first you must have something to eat.'

I pictured a bowl of mincemeat and then saw it land in front of me. But Billy couldn't get his head into the bowl very well, so I had to feed him by hand. By the end he seemed a lot better though, and I even conjured up some dog biscuits for 'afters'.

'Now, do you still want me to make your grave?' I asked.

'Yes, of course,' replied Billy. 'Then you'll know for certain I'll never bother you or your friends again. So follow me, as I've no wish to be buried here.'

Billy struggled to his feet and limped away. I followed him, trying to adjust to his very slow pace. And Billy led me into this wood. It was full of green trees and little clusters of flowers. And the sun was beaming down on us. I felt as if I'd wandered into a spring day.

'Where did this wood come from?'

I exclaimed.

'Oh, it's always been here,' said Billy, casually. But he wagged his tail at me as if sharing my pleasure in this beautiful place. Then he became sad and serious again. 'I'd like to be buried right here,' he said.

'All right,' I replied and rightaway I started to dig. It took much longer than I'd expected, and when I'd finished sweat was pouring off me.

'How's that?' I gasped. 'That's deep enough, isn't it?'

Billy staggered to the edge of the grave and peered down. Then he looked up at me. 'I never thought a human would do that for me.'

I smiled at Billy and patted him on the head. At once his tail started to wag again, only this time his tail was wagging so fast I feared he might fall over. I bent down and started rubbing his chest. He really liked that.

Finally, Billy looked up at me and said: 'I've wanted a grave for so long but now—I don't want to go.'

'And I don't want you to go,' I cried, holding on to him really tightly.

But the next thing I knew Mum was calling, 'It's half-past seven,' and Billy had disappeared.

CHAPTER EIGHT

'All right, everyone,' called Harry. 'Shut up a minute and raise your can of Coke to Dan for getting rid of the ghost dog. Two whole weeks have gone by and not one nightmare between us. Cheers, Dan.' Cans of Coke were clinked and I tried to look pleased.

We were in the hut: the place where it had all started, celebrating the fact that it was all over.

'Of course the ghost dog was Dan's fault. He called it up,' grinned Harry, 'trying to frighten poor old Aaron.'

'I seem to remember I wasn't the

only one trying to scare Aaron,' I said.

'Ah, but we're easily led,' replied Harry, his grin getting broader. He turned to Aaron. 'He made us do it, you know.'

'You all scared me something rotten,' said Aaron. 'And I can't tell you how good it is to sleep at night now. That's when I don't hear Dan whistling for Billy.'

I blushed. 'If you'd seen that dog and how badly it had been treated . . . and . . .'

'We know,' interrupted Harry. 'You told us once or twice,' and he gave a mock yawn. 'To be honest with you, Dan, I'm glad you can't find that dog. I'm really sorry for it but I don't want it popping up in any more of my dreams.'

'Or mine,' murmured Aaron.

Just then, there was a knock at the door.

'It's the ghost dog,' joked Harry.

Instead, my mum walked in, smiling nervously. 'I'm sorry to break up the fun, but I do need to have a word with Aaron and Daniel tonight.'

'Come on, what have they done?' cried Harry.

'Nothing,' I said, indignantly, before adding, 'Have we?'

'No, it's not a telling off,' said Mum.

'Shame,' muttered Harry.

Mum returned to the house, closely followed by Aaron and Harry. Laura waited for me.

'You're very quiet,' I said to her.

'Mmm.'

'What's up?'

'I've just been thinking,' she sighed, 'about the ghost dog . . . Billy. Maybe it's for the best. He wasn't very happy here, was he?'

'He was happy with me.'

'But you gave him what he wanted,' said Laura. 'You made him a grave.'

'Yeah, but . . . every night I'm in that churchyard, you know, whistling and calling for him. I know he's probably gone, but I'd really like to find him.'

Laura didn't answer. She just gave my hand a squeeze.

Inside the house Aaron was waiting for me. 'What do you reckon this is about?' he asked.

'I don't know. It doesn't feel like one of Mum's lectures, but you never know.'

'I bet she's heard from Dad,' said Aaron.

Mum was in the lounge. 'Have you heard from Dad at all?' asked Aaron cheerily.

'Yes, I have. He'll be here tomorrow night,' said Mum.

'Great. I haven't seen him for ages,' began Aaron. Then he stopped. Mum was looking really upset about something.

'What's wrong?' I asked.

'The thing is,' said Mum, slowly, 'Roy and I have decided to part. It hasn't been working out, so we both decided it would be for the best for all of us.' She paused. Aaron and I were too stunned to know what to say. 'So Roy will be arriving tomorrow evening to collect Aaron.' I just hated the way Mum said 'collect Aaron'. She made it sound as if Roy were popping round to pick up a parcel—not a person.

'Can't I stay a bit longer, until the end of term anyway?' asked Aaron.

'Roy wants to make a clean break,' said Mum in that same slow tone. 'He's picked out a school in America—a

128

really good school—and they're happy to take you rightaway, so you can have Christmas in your new home.'

I shook my head in amazement. 'I can't believe this.'

'We will try and make sure you and Aaron still see each other,' said Mum.

'I reckon we will,' I cried, 'with Aaron in America and me here.'

'It won't be easy,' agreed Mum. 'But we'll arrange something. Roy and I will still be friends, of course . . .'

'Just like you and Dad are,' I snapped. Straightaway I wished I hadn't said that. Especially as Mum looked as if she was about to burst into tears. But I was angry and upset and I had to hit out at someone.

Actually, I think Mum knew that, because she said, quietly, 'I'll miss Aaron too, you know.'

*　　*　　*

Aaron and I sat up talking most of the night. We decided to tell Roy that Aaron didn't want to move away from here, and that was that.

129

But when Roy arrived he was so determined, so obviously eager to get this over with, it was impossible to reason with him. Roy did promise Aaron this would be the last change he'd have while he was at school, but that was all.

Finally, all of Aaron's stuff was packed away in Roy's car.

'Are you sure I can't make you a cup of tea or something?' asked Mum.

'No, no, best be off,' said Roy. 'Traffic's building up.' Roy gave Carrie a hug, shook hands with me and told me 'to look after Mum', after which he gave Mum the tiniest kiss you'd ever seen, looked embarrassed and wandered out to the car. Aaron and I shook hands.

'We wasted so much time,' I said.

'Oh, well, these last two weeks . . . best of my life,' said Aaron. We shook hands again. 'Say goodbye to Laura and Harry for me, won't you?' said Aaron, his voice growing thicker.

'Sure.'

'And Rocky.'

I sprang up. 'I'll get Rocky now,' I said. I brought Rocky downstairs and he immediately jumped on to Aaron's shoulder.

'See you then, Rocky,' croaked Aaron. He had his head lowered, but there was no hiding his tears.

'Aaron's crying,' whispered Carrie.

'Sssh,' muttered Mum.

That night my bedroom seemed very large and very empty. I'd got used to Aaron being there and chatting and having a laugh with him. I remembered what he'd said to me as he left: 'These last two weeks have been the best two weeks of my life.'

They had been the best two weeks of my life too. And now I had to get used to being on my own again. No more Aaron. I buried my face in the pillow and let some tears escape.

That was three weeks ago. Today I got my first letter from Aaron. He told me all about his new school and home. Then, right at the end, he asked about the ghost dog. He'd never seen it since. Had anyone?

Well, Laura and Harry haven't, although I think Laura would half-like to see him.

But I have.

It happened the night Aaron left, actually. I was whistling for him, just as I'd done all those other nights. Then suddenly I cried out, 'Billy, have you really gone? Oh, where are you?'

'I'm right behind you,' said a voice. And there he was. I couldn't believe it.

'But where have you been?'

'I haven't been far away,' said Billy.

'But didn't you hear me calling you all those other nights?'

'I was hiding,' said Billy.

'Hiding!' I exclaimed.

'You humans have a way of creeping into a dog's heart,' said Billy. 'This time I had to be sure.'

'And now?'

Billy didn't reply. He wagged his tail a lot, though, then said, 'Come on, we're wasting time.'

And he led me back to that amazing wood. I fed him there. He was much hungrier this time and his wounds were healing up well. In fact, he said he was feeling so much better he wanted me to throw him some sticks.

So I threw the sticks a little way and Billy proudly brought them back. Then we talked and talked and the sun shone through the trees the whole time. It was just brilliant.

And when I could feel the dream starting to fade I called out, 'Billy, don't hide from me again, will you?'

'Whistle for me and I'll be there,' he called back.

And I know he will. Not as the ghost dog. But as himself, BILLY.

You couldn't dream about a better dog.